Anonymous

Edmar and Elwinna: or, The Woer-warlock

An old Ballad, but Never Before pPublished

Anonymous

Edmar and Elwinna: or, The Woer-warlock
An old Ballad, but Never Before pPublished

ISBN/EAN: 9783744773089

Printed in Europe, USA, Canada, Australia, Japan

Cover: Foto ©Andreas Hilbeck / pixelio.de

More available books at **www.hansebooks.com**

EDMAR AND ELWINNA:

OR,

THE WOER-WARLOCK.

AN OLD BALLAD,

BUT NEVER BEFORE PUBLISHED.

EDINBURGH:

PRINTED FOR AND SOLD BY THE BOOKSELLERS.

MDCCXCIII.

ADVERTISEMENT

BY THE

E D I T O R.

THE manuſcript of the following ballad was, along with ſome other old pieces, both in verſe and proſe, written by the ſame author, put into my hands by my grandfather two or three years ago. Not that the old gentleman (who is ſince dead) had any thought of publiſhing them : He was a man that, while he cared more for the antiquity of his family than for poetry, prized alſo golden more than literary treaſure, and perhaps had never looked into them. Their age gave them all their value to him. He had been informed that I, who was his favourite, made verſes; and, having ſent for

me

me one day, he advifed me to give over fo idle and dangerous a practice, as he called it; but concluded his advice with telling me, that, if I liked metre, he would fhow me fomething curious in it. Away he went, and returned with the old pieces I have mentioned. They were written, he faid, by an anceftor of the family, who was a fchoolmafter, and lived, he was fure, feveral generations ago, but how many he could not tell.

THE only piece among them, that feemed to be worth printing, was the ballad now prefented to the public. But its language was fo old, that it would have been to by far the greateft part of readers as if written in a foreign tongue: Its ftyle, too was uncouth. I, therefore, thought, though perhaps fome antiquaries will think otherwife, that it would be doing but juftice to the poem;—and what the author himfelf, could the old carle have rifen from his cold couch after a fleep of two or three centuries to be

his

his own editor, would have done,—to modernize it, (ftill, however preferving its character), and fo render it not only intelligible to all, but to the generality more pleaf-ing. Thus I thought, and I have acted accordingly. Yet, though, I confefs, I have made free with the MS. in chang-ing the old fpelling to the modern, in fubftituting Englifh words for Scottifh ones, which were now fo obfolete that they would have hurt the reading, in altering expreffions, that were pedantic or had too much of the rude boldnefs of " other days," in fmoothing rugged lines, and in mak-ing rhymes more exact, I have meddled with none of the fentiments. The ballad's character is ftill entire, and its antiquity ftill very evident.

EDMAR AND ELWINNA:

OR,

THE WOOER-WARLOCK.

I.

FAST by the rill, that feem'd to talk,
  ('Twas merry May's fweet time,)
Liftening fhe ftood, in beauty's beft,
  Stood, like all round, in prime.

II.

O, fure fhe is a maid fo fair,
  Her fairer fwain ne'er woo'd!
And blithe is fhe, to fmiling giv'n,
  But what is better, good;

A

III.

III.

For never yet could fhe think ill,
    Mild as the nun and true.
Her form is of the figure *jimp* *.
    Her eyes they are fo blue!

IV.

I'll tell fhe is fo noble' a dame,
    (Nor tell I it through pride,)
'Twould much befeem, ay, our Scotch king †
    To fit by her fair fide.

V.

And *eaft* ‡ fhe looks, and *weft* § fhe looks,
    And to the north and fouth,

Now

---

* *Jimp figure* is flender make.
† One of our Jameses without doubt, but which of them I have no authority to fay.
‡ Eaftward.
§ Weftward.

Now whom, deem ye, fhould fhe look for
    But Edmar, happy youth?

VI.

Full much fhe feels within her heart,
    Full much fhe thinks in mind,
But fhort while turn her cares all day
    From Edmar good and kind.

VII.

And this, wot ye, is Venus' eve *,
    The prime of eves to love ;
Hearts are both fooner fix'd its tide,
    And fix'd, they ne'er more move.

VIII.

Now why comes not my true-love ? why ?
    He *tryfted*† me 'gainft eve
To meet him on this green-grafs bank,
    To hear love, and believe.

IX.

* Friday eve.
† Made an appointment with. This is not juft the exact meaning
of *tryfted* here, but I cannot wel! find words to explain it better.

IX.

Yet fure, by my proud fide, ere long
  Shall he thofe troutlings view,
If heaven forbid all harm to come,
  For aye his lips were true.

X.

With this her anxious eyes look round,
  (And they are twins ftar-born,)
Look up the *haugh*, * look down the haugh,
  Which hazel trees adorn.

XI.

A native fear that dwells in them
  Prays aye, (and wins th'implore,)
Good Powers! guard me, for I'm felf-weak!
  But now this three times o'er.

XII.

* A *haugh* is a low piece of ground on the banks of a ftream.

XII.

And at each *foughing* * of the leaf
  She turns, and thinks to fpy
The coming of her bonny *joe* † :
  And aye is heav'd the figh.

XIII.

Long, long fhe waits, and fore fhe longs,
  Yet cannot wifh's power
Find of her love more than when firft
  She came, before the hour.

XIV.

When lo ! with reverend ftep, full flow
  Defcends the haugh a wight

B   Of

---

* A *fough* is a foft found ; to *fough* is to found foftly, &c. But indeed *fough* conveys an idea through Scottifh ears, which to exprefs in words is difficult. It is pronounced by the more polifhed fwains as if written *fouff*.

† Sweetheart, friend, &c.

Of ancient form.—Now, ween ye, who
    Comes on her boding fight?

XV.

Bent down, like withered branch, he comes :
    A ftaff ftays up each hand.
His coat and gloves are of the *gray**
    Weav'd in the fair Mers-land.

XVI.

And girds his loins a leathern zone,
    (Its buckle-band is fpy'd);
While coal-black is his bonnet broad,
    No ribbands give it pride.

XVII.

And O, full long and fnowy too,
    The fign of eighty years,

Waves

* Coarfe cloth, called fo from its colour; and alfo *natural gray*, from its being made of white wool mixed with black, not dyed by the hands of man, but of *Nature*, or the produce of the black fheep.

Waves down his beard! The warlock-wight
Ah! much Elwinna fears!

XVIII.

Now Chrift be with me! thrice fhe prays,
   'Tis Glorloz of the *knoww* * *!*
And thrice is crofs'd her bofom white,
   And thrice is crofs'd her brow.

XIX.

Our loves, our loves (Ah! how it bodes!)
   Shall Evil's face fee firft,
Since, for my joe, the firft I've fpy'd
   Is warlock, pilgrim worft.

XX.

And fhe hath tripp'd, yet trembling much,
   To pafs him on the *right*,
And fpeak the *firft* word, all his fpells
   To break, ay, in his fpite :

* Steep, or rather hillock.

XXI.

For warlocks' fpells may broken be
   By fpells of Chriftian men.
(Be then not fearful, though ye meet
   The ill wight in the glen.)

XXII.

Thrice hail! thou carle of knowledge deep!
   Thrice hail! command thou me!
Thrice hail! I crave for boon thy grace!
   And on his right ftands fhe.

XXIII.

And happy now fhe is, I trow,
   For fpells can do no ill:
When coughing thrice, and breathing faft,
   The warlock ftays him ftill.

XXIV.

Then lifting flowly up his neck,

It

(It *dows* * not climb fo high
But that his bonnet fhades his eyes)
He flowly makes reply :

XXV.

Hail, daughter fair ! (for fair art thou
As e'er won young man's heart !
Mine eyes are veil'd with age, but this
My fpells to me impart.)

XXVI.

My boon to thee fhall be my grace,
If thy foft arm of youth
Will ftay my weary frame of eld,
And if thou wilt tell truth.

XXVII.

Sore quakes the maiden to hear this ;
Yet forer to gainfay :

C   So

* To *dow*, I think, is to be able to find in one's felf to do.

So muttering thrice, O Chrift fhield me !
　She muft prepare t'obey.

XXVIII.

When (thrice now crofs'd her bofom white,
　And thrice her lovely brow,)
She fees one arm hide it in glove,
　And one its charms avow.

XXIX.

And wots fhe not that things *unlike*
　To evil's Lord pertain ? *
The taper limb (like fnow of morn)
　Soon the pleas'd air doth gain.

XXX.

Her *left* hand now fhe trembling puts
　Beneath the fpell-wight's arm ;
But then, o'er it, the rival right
　Forms *crofs* to keep from harm.

XXXI.

* This line ftands in the MS. thus,
　　　　Are dower of evil's thane.

XXXI.

And in her fhaking heart fhe fays,
  Would fragments were with me
Of Chrift's dear tomb, or Mary's houfe,
  Borne to beft Italy!

XXXII.

Now *fonfe* * befal thee, daughter true,
  For this true daughter's deed !
And for thy love I'll give a boon ;
  Thy fortune, child, I'll read †.

XXXIII.

This hand fhall blefs a youth, whofe heart
  Is love up to the brim.
Six fons, full brave, and daughters fix,
  Full fair, fhalt thou give him.

XXXIV.

* That which is good, fortunate, &c.

† To *read the fortune* of a lady (for inftance) among the Scots, is to foretel it by reading it in magic charaɛters.

XXXIV.

Your loves ſhall be the wonder ſtill
   Of all the caſtles round:
So charm'd, each ſwain ſhall haſte to wed,
   Each maid be willing found.

XXXV.

And ye ſhall live (and live aye bleſt)
   Till nought your eyes can ſpy.
Your ſons' ſons' ſons ſhall round the couch
   Stand weeping, when ye die.

XXXVI.

Now tell thy fire, O ſtar-lov'd dame !
   (I charg'd thee to be true)
If in this mead lurks Edmar young,
   His coat and bonnet blue.

XXXVII:

For he hath wrought me mickle ill ;
   And hither, at this hour

Of

Of eve, have crawl'd my rigid limbs,
　　With all my fpells of power.

XXXVIII.

And well can I full mickle ill
　　Work him, O virgin dame !
For I was born the *feventh* fon :
　　And Glorloz is my name.

XXXIX.

I'm cunning in the lore of ftars ;
　　And me, to aid, have fworn
Their numerous fprights, (whofe power fways all),
　　While prickly grows the thorn.

XL.

And hear : Who works dread Glorloz ill,
　　Shall not on Venus' eve
Begin his love ; and love begun
　　Shall but his bofom grieve.

D　　　　　　　　　　XLI.

XLI.

His flocks and herds no more fhall thrive;
　His health fhall thrive no more;
No more his babes; but he fhall fade
　As fnow when rills run o'er.

XLII.

And at the hour of fiends, his couch
　Shall fee ftill fights of blood;
And hear ftill fearful groans and yells;
　And naught fhall work him good.

XLIII.

Now tell with truth, O lady fair!
　(And telling, be full loud;
Few founds now pafs mine ears, grown dull
　With age, that makes me proud),

XLIV.

If in this meadow hides himfelf,
　Falfe Edmar, as I ween:

For

For fiercely burns my warlock-ire,
  And ill fhall it be feen.

XLV.

With angry tone the warlock threats
  While trembles *lith* * and limb
Elwinna ; and the more fhe thinks,
  The peril looks more grim.

XLVI.

I knew, I knew much ill was nigh
  Our loves, foon as I fpy'd
The ominous wight, a warlock, for
  The true knight of my fide !

XLVII.

And pearl-like ftands the molten woe
  Upon her brow of love :
Yet, from the crofs, to wipe, dares not
  Her fnowy right hand move.

XLVIII.

* Joint.

XLVIII.

Good Chrift ! forbid his warlock-fpells
  To work my Edmar harm !
And king art thou, ev'n warlocks fear !
  No fpell can ftay thine arm !

XLIX.

Low prays fhe thus; then fadly wails :
  Why wouldft thou do him wrong ?
Why wouldft thou work fweet Edmar ill,
  The beft that e'er was young ?

L.

How can it be that thou can'ft find
  Within thy heart, O fire !
To harm a one fo goodly good —
  O' *ilka* * heart's defire !

LI.

He holds his vaffals as his fons :
  And to his *lairdly* † hall

Crawls

---

  * Every.   † Lordly.

Crawls in, ay, many a pilgrim bent,
  But out come dancing all.

LII.

Then, much he grieves to hunt the hare,
  And oft would ftay behind ;
And when he hooks the pretty trout,
  He fore relents in mind.

LIII.

O how, then, would he e'er work ill
  To beard and locks like thine ?—
I tell thee, daughter, he hath wrought
  Me mickle ill in mine.

LIV.

For, at the foot of Dirring-hill,
  My fon dwells, true though low :
The *hether* * caps his clay-built cot,
  Blithe fwain—nay, now not fo.

E

* Heath.

LV.

For, dame, he hath a daughter fair,
    And he hath only one,
All fimple, as the bouncing lamb,
    And good : but fhe's undone. ·

LVI.

Ill Edmar fcour'd the heathy hills ;
    And, paffing near the gate,
He fpy'd the ruddy damfel, who
    On blue-ftone knitting fate.

LVII.

O ! but ye are a maid as fair
    As e'er look'd for the youth !
And will ye give me milk to drink,
    To cool my burning mouth ?

LVIII.

He afks in guile ; his mouth burns not :
    But he hath an ill aim ;

For

For in his wicked heart he'ath faid,
I'll lie with this fweet dame.

LIX.

And fhe hath raif'd her from the ftone,
And tripp'd it with good will ;
And foon the *double-lugged* * *quaigh*†
With the thick milk doth fill.

LX.

Now, blufhing, fhe hath giv'n the difh;
But not to him her eyes,
Which from her foot unfhod, that ftrokes
The hether, dare not rife.

LXI.

He drinks, and breathes, and drinks again :
Such beauty, damfel bright,

Was

* Double-eared.

† A *quaigh* is a round wooden difh with two cars.

Was ne'er made for this cot obfcure,
  But to give laird's hall light.

LXII.

And fits your fire within the cot?
  Or doth your mother fpin?
My fire he feeds the far off flocks;
  My mother's not within.

LXIII.

For fhe hath fped her to the fair,
  To fell her rural ftore;
And, fir, I ftay to tend the cot,
  At home there's no one more.

LXIV.

He's glad, and lights foon from the fteed,
  Which ties he to the gate;
Then clafps the maid and kiffes her,
  All blufhing and full *blate* *.

LXV.

* Bafhfu!,

LXV.

*Syne** he hath led her to the couch,
  And luftily talks love,
While dreadful things he prays may come,
  If ever he falfe prove.

LXVI.

Full fix moons, now, and one have fhin'd,
  Ay, fince the filly dame
Was maid no more ; but, day by day,
  Bedew'd her ruin'd name.

LXVII.

For now fhe's like a faded flower :
  Men fling it to the mire,
Though on its ftem it charm'd each eye,
  And made each breaft afpire.

F

LXVIII.

* Then ; after that.

LXVIII.

The pride of virgin purenefs gone !
  Gone chaftity divine !
Now fwains, that erft fued at her feet,
  To trample her would join.

LXIX.

And often at the dead of night
  She cries along the heath,
Sweet Chrift ! give both the babe and mè
  To the bleft cave of death !

LXX.

But ere fleep ftretch me, fure fhall gripe
  The perjur'd wight my fpells.—
Now, fire, 'tis not *my* Edmar : no,
  But fome wrong'd maiden's elfe.

LXXI.

I ken it clearly from thy tale :
  O! how can it be he,

Who

Who hath fo often kneel'd and fworn,
   He ne'er lov'd one but me ?

LXXII.

And now (though much my bofom feels
   The weeping maid's fad plight)
If not my Edmar's was the ill,
   My Edmar's why the wite * ?

LXXIII.

For if another did the wrong,
   And mark'd him with the brand,
Could my love, he, prevent the deed ?
   Or who fcapes Falfehood's hand ?

LXXIV.

Would e'er he make a maiden good
   An ill one, and defpif'd ?

Or

* Blame. The editor thought *wite* Scottifh, till he found it in Spen-
fer. That fine old bard has feveral words which, though now obfolete
in England, are ftill generally ufed in Scotland.

Or fo turn all her joy to woe,
  The grave were all fhe priz'd ?

LXXV.

Then, too, our mutual love began
  On day, by Venus ow'd *.
And knew'ft thou him, he's good and true
  As e'er was prieft of God.

LXXVI.

O me ! he's fweeter than the milk
  That reeks yet in the pail !
And fofter than the molten pearl
  That decks each morn the dale !

LXXVII.

Yet, as our Wallace, brave is he,
  And fierce 'gainft each falfe foe ;
Then, gallant as the pilgrim knight,
  That frees wrong'd dames from woe.

LXXVIII.

* To *owe* has here the old fenfe of to poffefs; to be the owner of;
to own.

LXXVIII.

He's lovelier than maid's tongue can tell,
  Or maid's eye wifh to fee :
And he 'ath ne'er lov'd, nor e'er will love,
  O fire! but only me.

LXXIX.

Now tell me nought, O daughter dear!
  Of all his charms fo rare,
Or of the oaths he 'ath fworn to thee :
  Thy words are words of air.

LXXX.

What's bonnier than the freckled fnake?
  What's fair as fnow to view ?
What's fweeter than the finging bourn * ?
  What nobler than the yew† ?

G   LXXXI.

* Rill.

† The *yew*, it would feem, has loft its fame fince the mufket fup-
planted the bow.

LXXXI.

The firſt hath many ſtung to death ;
  The ſecond many ſtarv'd ;
The third hath drown'd th' uncautious maid ;
  The fourth foul murderers ſerv'd *.

LXXXII.

O, ſimple fair ! didſt thou think right,
  Or know the ways of youth ;
The bonnier is the wanton wight,
  The viler is his truth.

LXXXIII.

And what the common oaths of love
  From men?—words, to work ill ;
Wiles, to win each his ſilly maid
  (Too waxen) to his will.

LXXXIV.

* It is a common ſuppoſition, that the yew contains a deadly poi-
ſon.

LXXXIV.

For, while their lips found awful words,
  Thus fays their bofom's drift,
To break love-oath's fo venial fin,
  We'll tell it not at fbrift *.

LXXXV.

As witnefs (to a grandfire's woe)
  The oaths that wrought the fhame
And ruin of my pride and hope,
  And blow my fury's flame.

LXXXVI.

Yet deem thou not, O precious maid !
  I think thy Edmar blithe,
The Edmar that hath rous'd mine ire,
  Which foon full ill fhall *kythe* †.

LXXXVII.

* Confeffion.   † Appear.

LXXXVII.

To ken this give me not my fpells ;
; But lift, and learn from me
The Edmar that hath hated mine,
    And tell if this loves thee.

LXXXVIII.

Ill Edmar is an only fon,
    And lives i' th' fair Mers-land.
Wide are his fields, nor few ; the flocks
    Many that wear his *brand* *.

LXXXIX.

Brown are the locks that fhade his back ;
    And peat-brown are his eyes.
He loves a maid—on fairer, no,
    The fun did never rife.

XC.

* Diftinctive mark put on fheep.

XC.

Her name—the one is mufic, he
  Sings coming from the chace !—
Gay fmiles fit thronging in her look
  As in their chofen place.

XCI.

And flax-fair are the treffes long
  That feek her bofom white.
Her voice, none fweeter charms the Spring :
  Her eyes—what blue fo bright ?

XCII.

Dame, thou haft feen the azure veil
  Round Cheviot's brow of fnow,
Weav'd by the fun in ether's loom,
  More bright their blue, I trow.

XCIII.

When fond proud youngling Smiles would try
  Her lovely mouth * to ope,

H   To

* *Her lovely mouth*; in the MS. Her mouth's bleft bower.

To show two flocks of snow-white twins.

(And temperance gives them hope.)

XCIV.

In mould how fair Heav'n cast her form !
    Nor had ill Art the soul,
With fingers rude, to dare to spoil,
    Or Heaven's own aim controul.

XCV.

If fair her form, as fair her mind,
    Ay, fairer, hold me true :
She's constant as the cooing dove,
    She's full as gallefs, too.

XCVI.

Now, she an only daughter is ;
    And her white flocks are seen
By those of the false Edmar, wot :
    One rill runs down between.

XCVII.

On Venus' eve, along the mead,
    With bow unbent, came he ;

Nor

Nor thought of love, but on his hounds,
  Or making *forayers* * flee.

XCVIII.

So Edmar came,—when on his eyes,
  From out a hazle-bower,
Tripp'd forth the maid, how bright! He ftood—
  What fill'd his foul that hour!

XCIX.

What heed I feud! what, family-rage?
  Th' eternal pact fhall make
A lady of fuch beauty mine!
  Life's worth but for her fake!

C.

He 'xclaim'd: then, keeling, told his love.
  She blufh'd; and to him faid,
If ye love me, O, I love you.
  And that bleft eve was made

CI.

* Robbers on the borders, fo named from *foray*, which fignifies a plundering incurfion; and is probably a provincial corruption of *forage*.

CI.

The mutual vow, to love till death :
    And oft hath Edmar chide
Slow Time, that will not hafte and give
    His arms fo fair a bride.

CII.

And one day late the fire of each
    Laid in the cell of death,
While their aye-jarring feud through life,
    With them gave up its breath,

CIII.

To be inhumed in the couch
    Of their join'd houfes' heirs.
And lift! this eve (my fpells fhow me)
    This meadow Edmar bears,

CIV.

Come to hear wrong'd Elwinna's love,
    Told in love's own pure ftyle.—
And is my Edmar falfe to me?
    And is my Edmar vile ?

CV.

CV.

The crofs disjoints ; and fhe had fall'n
  Straight down upon the mead,
But that with care the gray carl's arms
  Stay her in time of need.

CVI.

Oh ! from this hour forth, never more
  Will I go through my gate !
Farewell for aye mine ancient hall !
  And maids that on me wait !

CVII.

For I will hie me to the dame
  Whofe wrongs lone Dirring hears ;
And as we have been like in woes,
  We fhall be like in tears.

CVIII.

We'll weep within the cot by day,
  And wet the heath by night ;

I

Till

Till Death fhall ftretch us in one tomb,
 And make our wrongs all right.—

CIX.

Now fpeak not thus, my daughter lov'd ;
 Why tak'ft thou evil fo?
O! truft my years, knows its own pains
 'The *lairdlieft* * blifs below.

CX.

And what boots whining grief? ray, it
 Alone makes fuffering fore.
The milk once fpilt upon the pool
 Can ne'er be gathered more ;

CXI.

The ftone once tumbled from the hill
 Can ne'er climb up again :
Then for why deeds can ne'er b' undone
 Should fhe that's wife complain?

CXII.

* Lordlieft.

CXII.

In footh that is the why I wail;
    For O ! could deeds b' undone,
Hope would fhine through my darkfome breaft,
    As through dark clouds the fun.

CXIII.

But deeds, once done, are done for aye ;
    So aye muft be my woe :
And grief, not comfort, give thy words.—
    To Dirring-hill I'll go.

CXIV.

But loofe thou firft my leathern zone,
    (Unlock the buckle band),
And eafe me of my coat of gray,
    That lightened I may ftand,

CXV.

To go to feek ill Edmar out,
  · And forrow on him lay,

Worfe

Worſe ſorrow than he 'ath laid on thee.—
   O ſire not ſo, I pray !

CXVI.

I pardon all he'ath laid on me;
   Nor e'er can wiſh him pain :
And too thy ſon's wrong'd child will join
   His ſafety to obtain.

CXVII.

True he hath done much wrong to her;
   So hath he done to me.—
Pluck off my gray, thou matchleſs maid,
   And good ſhall come to thee.

CXVIII.

Now, ſhe doth tremble limb and lith
   To give an aiding hand
To warlock bent to harm her joe,
   Yet dare ſhe not withſtand.

CXIX.

CXIX.

And fhe hath loos'd the leathern zone;
   And fyne the coat of gray
She hath ta'en by the right-hand fleeve,
   The carle to difarray,

CXX.

And now the bonnet black (with locks
   Of age) is toff'd behind;
While chefnut locks, no ftunted length,
   Fall curling in the wind.

CXXI.

Then from a foft unwrinkled chin
   The beard, fo fnowy feen,
Defcends, and fhows by Nature's hand
   It had not planted been.

CXXII.

And who now ftands before her gaze
   But Edmar, or a fhade

K

Of

Of Edmar, rais'd by fpells!   Thofe eyes?
  Now faints entreat for aid!

CXXIII.

The warlock hath put on the form
  Of Edmar to work ill!
O! break his fpells, great God of Heav'n!
  Nor let him win my will!

CXXIV.

But foon the youth the trembling maid
  Holds in his happy arms!
And preffing thrice her filken cheek,
  I'll guard thee from all harms!

CXXV.

No warlock's fpells have ftol'n my form,
  But I am Rofvil's fon.
O! free me from my falfehood feign'd,
  And pardon what I've done.

CXXVI,

CXXVI.

O me! 'tis my own Edmar's voice!
    My Edmar's voice again!
Ay, 'tis the Edmar's whofe true heart
    Shall ne'er caufe thine to plain.—

CXXVII.

And the ill Edmar I told of
    Is not thy Edmar, here,
But hard-foul'd Edmar of the hill,
    Who ne'er could fhed a tear.

CXXVIII.

Could e'er I wrong fweet woman fo
    As make fweet woman weep!
Could e'er I purchafe tranfient blifs
    With her long woe and deep!

CXXIX.

Could e'er I love, Elwinna, tell,
    Another maid than thee!
E'er feek to win another heart,
    When thine was kept for me!

CXXX.

CXXX.

I cloth'd me as a warlock-wight
  To hear thy matchlefs love.—
Thou'rt fairer than all maids below!
  Thou'rt good as all above!

CXXXI.

Now told I not, it was not you?
  For will I knew you true.
And ye will ne'er love none but me*;
  And I'll love none but you.

CXXXII.

So HYMEN tied th' eternal knot,
  (It was on Venus' day):
And long they liv'd, and aye lov'd well;
  And they were happy aye.

---

* Two negatives were very often ufed, by our fathers, to ftrengthen each other.

THE END.

www.ingramcontent.com/pod-product-compliance
Lightning Source LLC
Chambersburg PA
CBHW022204020726
47496CB00008B/2868